No More Worries

ELIZABETH BEST

Illustrated by Paul Harrison

The Story Characters

Ned
He worries
about everything.

Jess
Ned's dog.

Grandpa
Ned's grandfather.

Will
Ned's big brother.

The Story Setting

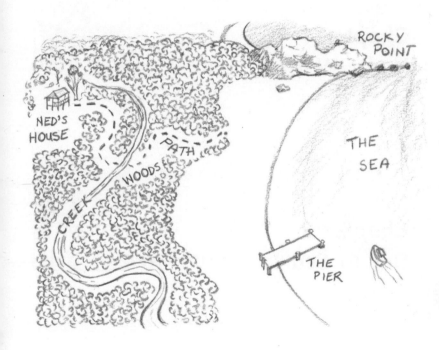

CHAPTER 1

Ned's Worries

Ned couldn't stop worrying. He worried about everything. If there was a test at school, he worried that he might fail.

"Worrying won't help," said Dad. "It only makes things worse."

"Sure, Dad," said Ned.

Ned's dog, Jess, gulped her food too fast. Ned worried that Jess would choke.

"Dogs always gulp their food," said his brother, Will.

"And pigs fly," said Ned.

When his mom and dad went out at night, Ned worried that they might get lost.

"We'll take a map," laughed Dad.

"What good's a map when you're lost, Dad?" asked Ned.

"When I grow up," Ned worried, "what if I'm a bad driver and have an accident? What if I don't know when to brake? How will I know where to go?"

"Relax," said Will.

He was no help.

Ned worried that his teacher would get angry with him.

"Don't do anything wrong," said Mom, "and you won't have to worry. It's simple."

"But how do I know what's right and what's wrong?" asked Ned.

CHAPTER 2

Out to Sea

The whole family was full of ideas, but nothing ever helped.

One Sunday, Grandpa was playing
cards with Ned. Grandpa saw Ned
was worried.

"Ned," he said, "if you have a worry, this is what you can do. Wrap the worry up and throw it far, far out to sea. You will never see it again."

Ned thought what Grandpa said
made sense.

So he waited for a big worry. It
wasn't long before one came along.

Next week, his school held a Field Day. Ned was going to be in a running race.

In bed that night, Ned worried. "What if I start running before the teacher says GO?"

"What if I come in last?"

Ned hadn't forgotten Grandpa's words.

"Wrap your worry up and throw it out to sea."

So he did. Ned put the worry in a brown paper bag. Then he put the bag in his backpack and took off.

"Come on, Jess," he called.

Ned and Jess cut through the woods at the back of the house. They climbed over rocks and jumped over a small creek.

At last they came to the beach. Ned threw his worry into the sea.

Grandpa was right. Ned stopped worrying and went home to sleep.

CHAPTER 3

The Worry Returns

But the next night . . .
the worry was back. What if I
trip and everyone laughs at me?

29

Ned told Grandpa, "I did what you said. But the worry is back. Worse than ever."

"What did you wrap the worry in?" asked Grandpa.

"Brown paper," said Ned.

"The paper got wet, and the worry got out. You need to use cloth," said Grandpa.

Ned Tries Again

That night when Ned saw the worry coming, he was ready.

He caught it and wrapped it in a
cloth bag. Then he put the bag in his
backpack.

Jess picked up the backpack in her teeth. The two of them crept out of the house.

They ran and ran. The woods were
full of scary eyes. They all stared at
Ned.

Ned's foot caught on a tree root, and
he fell over. There were thick vines
all around him. An owl hooted. Ned
got up and ran faster and faster.

At the beach, the sky was full of stars.

With all his might, Ned threw the worry into the deep water. Ned and Jess watched it sink.

But fish nibbled the cloth bag. The worry got out.

Ned Thinks Hard

"It didn't work, Grandpa. The worry is back."

"Enough is enough," said Grandpa. "It's your worry. You find a way to fix it."

Ned looked sad.

"You can do it," said Grandpa.

The next time, Ned put the worry in a box. He tied it with rope and threw it in the water.

A shark bit a hole in the box. The worry slid out of the hole, past the rope, and was BACK!

CHAPTER 6

Beyond the Horizon

Ned's brain began to flash fireworks. He was angry.

Ned shoved the worry into a metal
box. The box was very strong.
"Shark proof," Ned said to Jess.

Ned tied the box with heavy chains.
Then he put a padlock on the box.

Ned ran into the woods and down to the beach. Jess raced behind him.

This time, they ran to the pier at the end of the beach.

Standing at the end of the pier, Ned dropped the metal box into the dark, green water below. He and Jess watched it sink.

This time, Ned was sure the worry was gone. He'd done it.

Ned and Jess began the walk home along the beach.

Before they had gone far, the captain of a ship saw bubbles rising from the water.

The captain sent down a diver, who found the metal box. Once on deck, it was opened.

When Ned saw that worry back —
WOW, was he angry!

"I've had enough, Jess." he shouted.

Ned grabbed that worry and ran to the end of the pier.

He swung that worry around and
around, faster and faster. Then
faster still, until it was spinning at
a great speed.

He let it go. Away sailed the worry.

It flew across the waves. It flew over the dark water. It went beyond the horizon.

It landed with a thud on a boat
going to China. That worry was
never heard of again.

Ned came in first in the race. All of the running through the woods had made Ned fast.

Will came in last in his race.

"Too bad," said Ned.

"Why worry?" said Will. "It's only a race."

Ned knew what Will meant.

Ned has given up being a worrier.
But he still collects metal boxes,
pieces of rope, and a padlock or
two, just in case.

GLOSSARY

accident
an unlucky event
that happens
by chance

enough
as much
as you need

forgotten
not remembered

horizon
the line where the sea meets the sky

padlock
a lock with a key

pier
a wooden walkway
out over water

shark proof
stronger than the
shark's teeth

stared
looked hard at

Elizabeth Best

Elizabeth Best writes a bit of everything—adult short stories, children's stories, plays, articles, and novels. Best of all though, she enjoys writing stories for children. It is pure joy! Of course, Elizabeth doesn't really believe in throwing bags and boxes into the ocean.

Paul Harrison

Paul is an artist whose various roles as philosopher, teacher, and legal clerk have finally landed him in this, his finest role as an articulator of imagination. The tools Paul draws on are: a wry humor, a sense of fun, and occasionally a pencil.

Copyright © 2000 Sundance/Newbridge, LLC

All rights reserved. No part of this publication may be reproduced, stored in a retrieval system or transmitted in any form or by any means, electronic, mechanical,photocopying, recording, or otherwise, without the prior written permission of the publisher.

Published by Sundance Publishing
33 Boston Post Road West, Suite 440, Marlborough, MA 01752
800-343-8204
www.sundancepub.com

Copyright © text Elizabeth Best
Copyright © illustrations Paul Harrison

First published 1999 as Sparklers by
Blake Education, Locked Bag 2022, Glebe 2037, Australia
Exclusive United States Distribution: Sundance Publishing

ISBN 978-0-7608-4941-5

Printed by Nordica International Ltd.
Manufactured in Guangzhou, China
March, 2014
Nordica Job#: CA21400244
Sundance/Newbridge PO#: 227698